MASTER-MIND McGURK

This time the McGurk Detective Agency has a tough case—to hunt for a missing dog, a dog they can't even see! Join Jack McGurk on his hardest case yet as he and his partners match wits with the nine-year-old scientific genius—Brains Bellingham!

A McGURK MYSTERY #5

The Case of the Invisible Dog

by E.W. Hildick
Illustrated by Lisl Weil

AN ARCHWAY PAPERBACK
POCKET BOOKS . NEW YORK

To
Christopher and Michael Glynn
and their cousin,
Scott Webb

Contents

The Doughnut That Got Away

The first time we saw the invisible dog was just when we were about to begin the Mc-Gurk Organization's Annual Picnic.

Correction. . . .

That was the first time we *didn't* see the invisible dog, of course.

1

All we really saw was the doughnut as it went leaping and shaking and scudding through the grass, away from the table and into the bushes. At some points it would be on the grass, moving very fast. At other points it would be above the grass, moving even faster, flying along there about five or six inches from the ground.

It was unbelievable.

"Hey!" cried McGurk, through a mouthful of tuna sandwich. "What—?"

Then he trailed off, blinking hard.

"What's wrong?" said Willie Sandowsky. "You look like—"

Then he gulped. His peanut butter sandwich had been on its way to his mouth, but suddenly his hand jerked and the sandwich ended up right at the point of that long nose of his. He'd spotted the runaway doughnut, too.

"You *both* look like—"

Those were Wanda Grieg's words. She had a bunch of cheese-flavored tortilla chips in her hand and a smart gleam in her eyes. Then the gleam disappeared as she narrowed her eyes. She'd just caught sight of the bouncing, bounding doughnut as it went spinning through a gap in the bushes and into the next yard.

I was speechless. I wear glasses and I have to admit my eyes aren't very quick to focus, especially in the glaring sun. So although I was probably the first to see the doughnut— when it was only a few feet from the table —I thought my eyes were playing tricks and I kept quiet about it. Only when the others started yelling and gasping did I realize it was no trick of the sunlight. This was a real doughnut all right, seeming to move with a life of its own.

But let me describe the setup:
#1. The place: The end of McGurk's back-yard, with the picnic goodies all laid out on the table under a tree. The tree's trunk was to

the left of the table, and that was the only cover for a distance of twenty or thirty feet all around. But the doughnut was moving to the right, where there was nothing but rough short grass. So it was not as if some *visible* animal or a kid had reached out from a near-by bush and gone running off with it through tall grass.

#2. The time: Noon, on a bright summer day. There was nothing wrong with the light.

#3. The occasion: As I said, this was the McGurk Organization's Annual Picnic. We hadn't been in existence more than a few months, but that didn't stop McGurk from giving it the grand title.

"*Annual* picnic?" I'd said.

"Sure," McGurk had replied. "Why not? We've got four successfully solved mysteries to celebrate, haven't we? We deserve *four* annual picnics at that rate."

Well, it looked as if we had our *fifth* mystery to deal with now.

McGurk seemed to sense this.

"Quick!" he yelled, throwing down his sandwich. "Follow that doughnut!"

Wanda and I were the first to move. Mc-

Gurk and Willie were at the other side of the
table and had farther to go. But by the time
we reached the bushes that screened the next
yard, McGurk was in the lead.

"Oh!" he said, suddenly stopping.

This is where just writing a word down is not much good. I mean you ought to have been there to hear the way that one simple sound came from our leader's lips. When it began, it had a kind of yelping ring to it, like the sound a dog makes when someone treads on its paw. Then it slowed down some and deepened, like a dog when it hears intruders and gets very suspicious. But even that didn't last long, because next it faded into a puzzled whimper. Maybe it should be written down like this:

"OW-AAARRR-*ooop?"*

The reason?

Brains Bellingham.

Brains Bellingham was standing there, in the yard next door, with an impatiently wriggling little dog in his left hand, held by the collar, and a badly chewed doughnut in his right hand. The dog was Dennis, a Yorkshire terrier. He belonged to Miss Bellingham, Brains's aunt, who lived next door to the Mc-Gurks. The doughnut belonged to—well, Dennis, judging from the way he was straining to reach Brains's right hand.

"I'm sorry, McGurk," Brains said. "I didn't

mean for him to disturb your crummy picnic, really I didn't. But he just can't resist doughnuts, can you, Dennis?"

"Yip!" went the dog, making another pass at the remains of the doughnut. "Yurrr!"

"You see?" said Brains, putting Dennis down on the grass. "I've been getting to know him pretty well these past two days, while I've been staying with my aunt. My parents have gone to Chicago on business and—"

"I know *that!*" said McGurk, impatiently. "But—the doughnut—the dog—"

"Sure," said Brains. "That's what I was explaining. Dennis loves doughnuts so much I guess he'd even steal them. When he sees his chance. So—once again—I'm sorry for letting him loose just now. It was a pure accident."

Brains smiled apologetically. He really did look sorry. The eyes behind his large glasses were blinking rapidly and he didn't look directly at any one of us. And that in itself was unusual. As a rule, Brains stares you out: boldly and very critically, with the clear gray eyes of a very intelligent adult in his nine-year-old's face.

"But—but—"—McGurk's green eyes had a look of sheer bewilderment—"but—"

In the end, Wanda said it for him.

"But, Brains, we didn't *see* the dog. Just—just—"

Then it was her turn to run out of words.

"Just the doughnut," I said.

"Ba-barreling along in the grass," stammered Willie. "On—on its own."

Brains was looking more furtive than ever now. He stooped to the dog and patted it.

"Yes, well," he muttered. "Dennis is such a *small* dog—huh, boy?"

"Yip!" went Dennis, still gazing at the doughnut with eyes like shiny black grapes.

"And he—he kind of blends with his surroundings," said Brains. "You know. All this silky, grayey, bluey, kind of yellowy-browny hair. Like—uh—camouflage."

That was another thing that showed Brains was having problems: all that "uh-ing" and "you-knowing" and "kind-of-ing" stuff. He usually sounds like a page from an encyclopedia, without any fumbling.

We looked at each other. Could it be he was right? We looked at the dog, still straining after the doughnut, and I think we all shook our heads at the same time—every one of us. Dennis might very easily have blended into the background in long grass, at dusk. But not at this time of the day, even on McGurk's ragged lawn. No way.

"Hey, do you mind if I give him the doughnut now?" Brains said brightly, obviously trying to change the subject. "I mean it isn't fit to eat now, even for you guys."

This was more like the old Brains, always ready with a put-down.

But this time none of us felt like giving him an argument.

"Sure," murmured McGurk. "Go ahead."

We watched as Dennis caught hold of the doughnut in his teeth, shook it about for a few seconds from side to side, then lowered it to the grass and, growling with pleasure, began to eat it.

"You—you shouldn't give dogs sweet things," said Wanda, more for something to say than to criticize Brains.

"I know," said Brains. "But once in a while won't do him any harm, I guess. . . . Hey, listen. I think I heard my aunt hollering for me. Just keep an eye on him a minute, will you?"

We agreed. We were still stunned. We were still bewildered. The picnic itself had been forgotten for the time being. Back in McGurk's yard a whole pack of big, ravenous, slavering, plainly visible dogs could have been stealing the rest of the food, for all we might have known or cared.

"I just don't understand," said McGurk, staring at the dog. He's never even wandered into our yard before. Miss Bellingham's always bragging about it. Says he's the best-trained dog in the whole town."

"Yip!" agreed Dennis, looking up through his hair.

He'd finished with the doughnut now. About half of it lay on the grass in broken pieces.

"He's not greedy, anyway," said Wanda. She bent to pat him. His whole body quivered with pleasure, setting the metal tag on his collar jingling like a tambourine. "Bad—yes. But not greedy."

"Bad?" I said.

"Yes," she replied. "For coming into Mc-Gurk's yard and stealing the. . . ."

Then she trailed off—reminded of the problem again.

Dennis rolled over on his back. I inspected him closely. But it didn't help. He was just as visible from that angle, too.

Then:

"Hey, what's this?" said Willie.

He'd wandered off a little from the rest of us. He was bending over a large shiny black box. It was about eighteen inches high, two feet long, and eighteen inches wide.

Dennis gave a little yelp and went to join Willie. The dog sniffed at the side of the box and looked around at us, as if ready for a game. But by the time the rest of us had reached it we were more interested in the dials and levers and switches on the far side of the box. Much more interested.

"It looks like another of Brains's fancy inventions," said Wanda.

"Maybe a patent lawn mower," I said, smiling.

"Or a kind of super-modern kennel for the dog," said Willie. "You know. Air conditioning in the summer. Heating in winter."

"Yip!" went Dennis, standing on his back legs and scratching at the lid.

But McGurk was kneeling down, studying the dials and switches and reading the little plastic strips under them.

"Lawn mower, nothing!" he growled. "Kennel, my foot!" he snorted. "One of Brains's inventions—yes." He stood up. His face was pale. Every freckle stood out like a spatter of mud. His green eyes blazed with excitement. "Just take a look at what it says here!"

14

And what it said there, under one switch, was this:

Then McGurk's finger turned, trembling a little as it pointed to the label under the other switch:

"He—" McGurk took a deep breath. He closed his eyes and shook his head. When he opened his eyes he looked very perplexed— puzzled and pained at the same time. "He hasn't *really* found a way of making the dog invisible, has he?"

"Yip!" said Dennis, giving the lid another scratch.

2 Inside the Box

"Why don't we see what's inside the box?" said Wanda.

She was just being sarcastic, I guess, because McGurk already had the lid open. Dennis had put his front paws up on the edge again and was peering in with his black eyes bright and his stubby little pointed ears

17

cocked up, all alert. But what attracted the rest of us at first was not deep down inside the box. It was on the underside of the lid itself.

"Gosh!" whispered Willie. "It's like the works inside a radio."

"Or a television," I said.

"Something very complicated, anyway," said Wanda.

There were lots of colored wires there— blue and green and yellow—in neat loops and lines. There was a row of small silver batteries. Then there were things that only someone like Brains would be able to identify accurately—like rectifiers and timers and plugs and sockets and transformers and transistors, all joined together in different ways by the colored wires. And in the center of it all was a flat, round, pearly lamp, fixed so that when it was switched on and the lid was closed, it would send its rays straight down into the box.

"Don't touch!" snapped McGurk, as Willie's hand went near the controls. "There's no saying what might happen if one of those switches is pulled."

Willie drew back as if he'd been burned.

I turned my attention to the inside of the box itself.

It wasn't shiny like the outside. The box seemed to be made of a thin wood, and on the inside it was painted a dull black. At first I had thought it was completely empty, but as I peered closer I could see some small white things on the bottom.

I reached, but McGurk beat me to it.

"Crumbs" he said, pinching a few of them between his fingers and thumb. *"Doughnut* crumbs!" he added, as he brought them up into the daylight. "Right, Willie?"

To me they could have been bread or cookie or even cracker crumbs. But Willie has something more reliable than eyes for making such identifications.

He brought his great long nose close to McGurk's outstretched fingers, took a sniff, and nodded.

"Doughnut, all right," he said.

"Yip!" went Dennis—as if to say he could have told us that all along, if we'd only asked.

"Well," said Wanda, frowning thoughtfully, "it really does begin to look like—"

"Hey! Get out of there!"

This was Brains. He was striding down the yard from the house. His face was all red and sweaty and indignant.

"That's private!" he said, coming up and closing the lid.

"Sorry," said McGurk. "But—"

"Yeah! You look it! Always snooping, aren't you, McGurk? Always playing the big detective!"

Brains looked very bitter. Time and again he used to sneer at McGurk and the Organization like this, but he didn't fool me. I guessed it was jealousy really. I think what he wanted more than anything else was to join the Organization. Right at the beginning he had suggested it himself—though in a very roundabout way.

"What you *really* need is a laboratory man," he had said. "Someone who could make all the scientific tests of clues. Someone who could run the McGurk Organization's forensic science lab."

"The what?" Willie had asked.

"The forensic science lab. Forensic means to do with crime and law. Let's just say the *crime* lab then, if you dummies find it easier to pronounce."

Well, that was the trouble. Right there in those last few words. I mean, even though McGurk wanted to keep the membership down, we might have taken Brains on if it hadn't been for his uppity scornful attitude. I mean he'd only just turned nine—brains or no brains—and some of us are a whole year older than him, at least. As McGurk said:

"We don't want some smart-mouthed child bossing *us* around. And if there's any science work to be done, Joey here has the brains for it. So get lost, kid. Go invent yourself a new kind of candy."

Naturally, I felt very pleased about that remark. McGurk doesn't throw compliments like that around every day. But to tell the truth, I have to admit he was a bit off the mark there. English, geography, history, general intelligence—those are the kinds of things *my* brains are good at. Science and math—well, let's say I can get by in those subjects and leave it at that.

Brains Bellingham didn't. When McGurk paid me the compliment, the kid just looked at me through those big owl glasses and said:

"Brains for *science* work? Him? He wouldn't recognize a silicon-controlled rectifier if it bit him on the nose!"

The trouble was he was right, too. I wouldn't have.

Anyway, that's the way things were between us and Brains, and right now he was glaring at McGurk—acting real sore and just a bit worried.

"How long have you been poking your nose into my private property?" he said. "Huh?"

22

"Aw, come on, Brains!" said McGurk. (He could be polite enough when his curiosity was aroused.) "We didn't know it was all that private. We were only *looking* at it. What is it, anyway?"

This seemed to relieve Brains. His scowl relaxed. There was even a gleam of humor in his eyes when he replied:

"What *is* it? Why don't you ask your science expert, Professor Joey Rockaway there?"

Then his scowl returned as he stooped to pick up the box.

"Anyway, you're wasting your time. You ought to be getting back to your dumb picnic before the birds and the squirrels demolish it. Let's go, Dennis. *We've* got better things to do."

3 An Invisibility Machine?

After watching Brains go staggering up the yard with the box in his arms and Dennis jingling proudly at his heels, we returned to our picnic. Neither the birds nor the squirrels had interfered with the food on the table, but it wasn't the same as when we'd first started on the meal. We were all too puzzled by what we'd just seen.

McGurk did make one attempt to laugh it off.

"Brains thinks he's smart," he said, reaching out for a Devil Dog, one of his favorite foods. "But just watch me make *these* dogs invisible in *my* Invisibility Machine!"

This brightened us up a bit. We kicked the joke around a while with talk of Invisible *Chocolate Chip Cookie* Machines, or Invisible *Apple* Machines, or Invisible *Cheesecake* Machines—according to our own favorite foods. But it didn't help for long. This sort of joking made us realize the one big difference. I mean we may have been able to make these things disappear all right, but we sure couldn't make them visible again, the way Brains had made Dennis.

It was annoying, too. This was supposed to be a celebration picnic, remember. Yet here we were—slap in the middle of that celebration—squelched by a mystery we had no idea how to solve.

"Right, men!" said McGurk, as soon as we'd finished the food. "Let's clear all this junk away and get the table back into the basement. We have work to do!"

He didn't say what work. He didn't need to. We had just had a mystery dumped in our laps when we'd least expected it. The only thing we *could* do was get busy solving it. And that meant putting our Headquarters back into operational shape right away.

Ten minutes later, the table was in the basement where it belonged. My typewriter was back on it, and so were our files: the boxes labeled MYSTERIES SOLVED and CLUES and so on. And we were sitting around it, with McGurk in the old rocking chair at the head.

"Well?" he said, rocking angrily and staring around at us, one by one. "Any ideas? I mean what *did* happen to that doughnut? And what *did* happen to Dennis?"

"Personally," I said, "I think it was some kind of trick."

"So do I," said Wanda. She frowned, still very perplexed in spite of what she'd just said. "I mean—well—it just has to be. . . . Doesn't it?"

"Willie?"

McGurk was giving Willie a very fierce look.

"Well—well, I mean—well, I—I just don't *know*, McGurk! I mean—well—Brains *is* clever at things like that. Science things."

"Not that clever," Wanda said. "Right, Joey?"

McGurk cut in before I could reply.

"But he has invented some nifty little things, don't forget. Like his White Noise Machine, for drowning out other sounds at night, so he can get to sleep."

I nodded.

"Sure. I agree. But—an *Invisibility* Machine—?"

"He could have stumbled on it by accident, I suppose," said McGurk.

His eyes were very thoughtful—green slits among the freckles. He sat back and rocked.

"Yeah," murmured Willie. "Like—like the Chinese guy in that movie I saw. The one who invented gun-powder. That was an accident. Blew himself up with it."

Wanda groaned and looked at me. She didn't say anything, but I could guess what she was thinking. McGurk and Willie *wanted*

29

to believe in the Invisibility Machine. They were like that. I mean Willie was dumb enough and McGurk was—well, not dumb —but only too ready to believe in anything that made life interesting. Why, he even believed that there was something supernatural about Willie's nose—like it was not just an extra-sensitive sense of smell the kid had!

"The trouble with you, McGurk," I said, meaning to spell all this out, "is you're a sucker for any—"

Then I stopped.

Because that's when we heard the jingling. Like the tag on a dog's collar. But coming from inside, behind McGurk, in the other part of the basement, where the furnace is.

4 The Wet Bone

Now let's get this straight.

The door to the yard is in one corner of the basement, and the door to the furnace room is in the opposite corner. Our table, with us all sitting around it, was right between the two.

Now both doors were open that afternoon. It was very warm and we needed the air. But if any dog had crossed from one door to the other we would have been sure to see it. Any *visible* dog, I mean.

All right then. So was there another way into the furnace room?

Yes. Down the stairs leading from the main part of the house. But the door at the top of those stairs was shut. Mrs. McGurk always insisted on that, whenever we were down in the basement. Because of the noise we made when we got to arguing.

We were arguing now, as we stepped into the furnace room.

"I tell you it was just like the sound of a dog's metal tag!"

"But how could it be? There's no way a dog could have gotten past us."

"Maybe through a window."

"Window? What window, dummy? What kind of a dog could get through *these?"*

McGurk was right.

The basement windows were nothing more than ventilation slits really, about eighteen inches long and six inches wide. They were at ground level outside, and this meant they were way up at the top of the walls on the inside.

"Well, they're *open*," Willie said.

This was true. They were the sort that tilted inward a little way.

"Yes, but not wide open," Wanda murmured. "Only two or three inches. It would take a very *flat* little dog to squeeze through there."

"Yeah," said McGurk. "And it would be even flatter when it dropped from that height. But be quiet, all of you. It's *still* got to be in here somewhere, no matter how it got in."

This seemed true. We were all standing by the furnace room door. We fell silent and listened.

No jingling.

Only the sound of our own breathing.

Then the more raspy sound of Willie sniffing.

"Got something?" McGurk whispered.

Willie nodded.

"I smell dog," he said. "Fresh dog."

"That's my boy!" said McGurk, patting

him on the shoulder as if Willie himself were a dog. "Track him!"

It was dim in there. Apart from the furnace and its pipes and things, the room was cluttered with junk: old cartons of books, boxes of nails, broken blinds, bike parts, half-empty cans of paint that had set hard, a broken fan. That sort of stuff.

"It seems to come from over behind that stack of garden chairs," said Willie, leading the way.

We followed, straining our eyes, picking our way through the junk. There were plenty of places for a dog to be hiding in—but only if it could have made it into the furnace room without being seen.

So if it was a fresh dog smell, as Willie had said, it meant only one thing.

Suddenly, that one thing made me feel very creepy.

"Unbelievable!" I muttered.

"What?" said Wanda.

"Hah!" cried Willie.

He stooped so fast that his bony behind butted into McGurk.

34

"Hey! Watch what you're—" McGurk began.

Then he stared.

"See?" said Willie, triumphantly.

He straightened up.

He was holding something very daintily be-

tween finger and thumb. Something white. Something about five inches long, with lumps at the end.

"A—a bone?" whispered Wanda.

"Yeah," said Willie. "A rubber bone."

"Let me see that," said McGurk, snatching it from Willie's hand. "It's got writing on it."

It had. Here is an exact copy of the bone and its writing, which I made for our CLUES file.

The name was stamped on the rubber.

"Huh! It's just the brand name," said Wanda.

"I know that," said McGurk. "It isn't *that* that I'm examining. Look. Feel. It's still *wet!*"

It was, too. Wet and slightly sticky. Some dog had been chewing it fairly recently. This was no forgotten piece of junk, along with the scattered nails and old playing cards and the other stuff that littered the floor.

"Well," Wanda began, "it does begin to look—"

Then she broke off.

The jingling again.

This time it came from right behind us, in that same room, across at the other side.

We spun around. Stared. Peered.

Nothing.

There wasn't so much clutter on that side. No boxes or anything. Nothing for a dog to hide behind. Yet that was where the jingling had just come from.

Willie gave a little moan.

"I'm getting outa here!" he said, and made for the door to our part of the basement.

"Don't be such a—"

This was our day for not getting to finish what we were saying.

Because no sooner had McGurk caught up with Willie, reaching to grab him and haul him back to face up to his duties, than Brains called out:

"Hey, you guys! Seen anything of Dennis?"

He was standing at the outer door, at the foot of the steps leading up to the yard. He was blinking around at our Headquarters room with that same anxious look on his face.

"No," said Willie, still scared, "but we just *heard* something of him, and *smelled* something of him. An' I tell you, I don't like it, it's spooky, it—it—"

"It's time you cooled down!" snapped Mc-Gurk. "Get a hold of yourself, Officer Sandowsky!" He turned to Brains, who was still standing in the doorway. "Now. Let's get this clear. You say you've lost Dennis. What makes you think—?"

And that was yet another unfinished sentence, because just then something spookier yet happened.

Brains had been blinking around, as I said —but mainly at the floor, down by our feet, under the table, into the corners. Then all at once his eyes narrowed, and he began to squint, and he was looking down at the floor right in front of him, and:

"Gotcha!" he went.

He didn't yell it. He didn't whisper it. It was more of a muttered growl, coming from between his clenched teeth.

Then he made a grab, down by his ankles,

and although it looked like empty air he was clutching at, it sure didn't sound like it.

This was something else. This was thick, tough, turbulent air. Wriggling air. Snarling and growling and *jingling* air. I mean we heard it, all of us. We checked afterward and we agreed.

Those dog sounds—those struggling dog sounds—were loud and clear.

And they were coming from the space between Brains's clutching hands and his chest!

Suddenly he turned. Still clutching at this bundle of noisy nothing, he said, over his shoulder, in a strained voice that he tried to make calm:

"Oh, I think I hear Dennis now, up in the yard. Sorry to bother you, guys."

Then he ran up the steps, leaving us gaping at the door.

"I don't believe it!" whispered Wanda.

I'm not sure whether she meant she didn't believe what Brains had just said, or she didn't believe what we'd all just seen and heard. I didn't know what to think myself, and Willie looked like he'd faint if you just murmured "Bow-wow!" at him.

But McGurk's eyes were gleaming. *He* wasn't in any doubt.

"He heard Dennis all right," he said. "But it wasn't anywhere up in the yard. It was right *here*. In our Headquarters. In his arms. . . . Come on, let's follow him. But quietly, men. The silent approach."

5 Dennis Reappears

We did exactly that: followed McGurk, maintaining the silent approach. And when we reached the bushes we were just in time to see Brains putting that noisy bundle of nothing down into the box.

"All right, Dennis, all right!" he was saying, in low, soothing tones. "I'll have you visible again in no time. Just keep quiet and still."

McGurk turned to us.

"Hear that?" he whispered.

We nodded.

It was still hard to believe, but there seemed to be no other explanation.

"Let's tackle him," said McGurk. "He can't talk his way out of it now."

He led the way through the gap in the bushes, just as Brains was closing the lid.

"Hi, Brains!"

Brains gave a jump. He looked nearly as nervous as Willie had, back in the basement.

"Huh—what do you want?" he muttered, casting an uneasy glance down at the box.

There were now little whimpering, puzzled dog noises coming from inside.

"We see you found him," said McGurk.

"Eh? Who?"

Brains gave the lid a smack and the sounds trailed off.

"Come *on!*" said McGurk. "You know who."

"Dennis," said Wanda. "You have him in there, don't you?"

Brains blinked.

"Oh—him—you mean Dennis? Why—uh—no. No. I'm still looking."

Again that stumbling speech, so unusual for Brains Bellingham.

"Where?" jeered MuGurk. "In that box?"

"Eh? Here? In *here?* Why—why should I look in *here?*"

"Because you just put him in there, that's why!"

Brains shrugged.

"You must be nuts, McGurk. I mean *really* nuts. But see for yourself."

He opened the lid. We crowded around. The box was empty.

Completely, absolutely, positively empty.

Then McGurk said:

"Hi, Dennis! Good dog! Good boy!"

It worked.

From inside that empty black box there came a rustling sound, and a jingle, and a little friendly growl, and then a soft thumping, like the sound of a stumpy tail against wood.

Willie jumped back. Wanda and I weren't slow to follow. McGurk turned to Brains.

There was genuine admiration in his eyes as he said:

"All right, Brains. Stop trying to cover up. We *know*. You've really done it, haven't you?"

"Done—uh—what?" said Brains, closing the lid and looking suspiciously at McGurk over his glasses.

"Discovered a way to make things invisible."

Brains took a deep breath. He looked around at us, half annoyed, half anxious.

"Oh, well! I guess I can't deny it now."

Wanda was staring hard at him. I could tell she hadn't *quite* gotten over her own suspicions yet.

"So make the dog visible again, huh?"

Brains shrugged.

"Yes, all right. He's exceeded the period of maximum invisibility already." He glanced at the huge wristwatch he always wore: the one that told you the date, and the times in Hong Kong and London as well as the local time, and the phases of the moon, and the points of the compass, and all that sort of stuff. "He's exceeded it by three minutes and twenty-two seconds, so we'd better move fast. . . . Stand back, all of you, and keep absolutely silent."

We didn't argue this time. What he'd said about the invisibility period running over and

the way he looked made us feel we'd better obey him or something bad might happen to little Dennis.

So we watched in perfect silence as he

clicked switches on and off, pushed buttons, stared at the flickering needles on the dials, clicked more switches, pushed the buttons again (briskly now, like a clerk at a supermarket check-out), and finally turned a large lever—clockwise—through 180 degrees exactly.

Then he wiped the sweat off his forehead and looked at his watch, with his right hand held up to us, demanding we keep silent a little longer.

Then, when some precise number of seconds had passed, he reached out, unfastened the clasp, and threw open the lid.

"Yirr!"

That was Dennis, making a cheerful growling noise, as first his stubby ears, then his round black shiny eyes, and then his round black shiny nose appeared over the edge.

"Gosh!"

That was Wanda, convinced at last, as Dennis placed his front paws on the edge and gave himself a shake.

"Wow!"

And that was Willie, as Dennis clambered

out of the box and showed himself to be fully
visible again, from nose to wagging tail.

6 The Snag

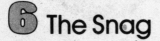

McGurk said it for all of us.

"Hey! Brains! That's some invention you've got there!"

His voice was full of admiration.

Brains smiled a little for the first time.

"Thanks," he said. "It's good of you to say

so." Then he went back to frowning. He took off his glasses and slowly polished them on the edge of his shirt. "But it's a long way from being perfect yet," he said, staring moodily at the box.

"How did you—I mean, how does it work?" Wanda asked.

She looked completely sold now, as she looked up from patting Dennis. The suspicious glint had left her eyes, and they were shining with wonder and trust.

"Well—" Brains shrugged. "I have to admit. It was an accident really."

"I told you!" said Willie, looking around at the rest of us. Even his *nose* seemed to be glowing with excitement. "Just like the Chinese guy!"

Brains gave him a puzzled glance.

"Whatever," said McGurk, anxious to get back to the point. *"How* was it an accident, Brains?"

"Well I'll tell you," said the young scientist. "You might as well know the full story now. . . ."

We listened in dead silence at first, while he told us. Dennis was the only one to make any sound. Whenever his name was mentioned, he wagged his tail, making his tag jingle. Or he'd give a deep little growl now and then, as if to say:

"That's right! That's exactly the way it was!"

It turned out that Brains had been aiming at a flea-killer.

"While I've been staying with my aunt, I decided to do something to get rid of Dennis's fleas and the ticks he's been picking up in the yard, in this hot weather. Now normally he wears a flea collar, and that does a pretty good job of getting rid of fleas and ticks. But it's a chemical process, you see. And the chemicals were giving him problems. A kind of allergy. A rash."

"Poor thing!" murmured Wanda at that point, picking the dog up and hugging him close, fleas or no fleas, rash or no rash.

"So anyway," Brains went on, rather dryly, "I figured I'd find a way to *solve* the problem. But *how?* Chemicals were out—obviously. Then I thought of light rays. Like you have ultraviolet lamps for skin problems. Maybe —I thought—maybe I could produce a ray

that would not only clear up the rash under his ears, but also kill off the fleas and ticks."

McGurk was nodding. He looked at the box.

"And that was it?"

"Yes. That was it," said Brains. "Instead of chemicals, a photoelectric process." Then he sighed again. "Trouble was, it made the *dog*

disappear as well as the rash and the ticks and fleas!"

"Gosh!" Wanda gasped. She'd released Dennis by this time, but now she had to pick him up for another hug. "I bet you flipped!"

Brains sniffed.

"I was somewhat concerned, yes. But I

went back to the circuit and made some changes, and—well—I was able to make him visible again."

"How about the fleas and things?" asked Willie. "Did they come back too?"

Brains shook his head; Dennis wagged his tail.

"No. *That* part of the invention was completely successful. No fleas. No ticks. Dennis doesn't need to wear a flea collar any more."

That reminded me. During all this talk, I'd been listening carefully, politely, respectfully. But I still wasn't one hundred per cent convinced, like the others.

"One thing, Brains," I said.

"Yes?"

He gave me a keen look. If this *was* a trick, he probably knew I'd be the one to see through it.

"How come we could hear the jingle of Dennis's tag if his collar was invisible?"

He smiled.

"Good question, Joey. But in the first place, his collar *wasn't* invisible. The machine only makes living tissue disappear. But tell me this. Can you see his collar *now,* when he *is* visible?"

"No," I said. "All that long hair covers it. But—"

"Right!" said Brains. "And when that long hair becomes invisible it *still* covers his collar. Don't ask me why. I don't know. It just does. I mean if Dennis was a short-hair breed you'd have seen the collar all right. You'd have seen this collar running around a few inches from the ground, and the tag jingling."

"Sure," said McGurk. "Like when we saw just the doughnut running around. I'm surprised at you, Joey. Asking dumb questions. . . . But I've got a more sensible one,

Brains. How come we hear Dennis himself, when he's invisible?"

Brains gave him a look that showed he didn't think much of *that* question, anyway.

"Because he's still *there*. You'd feel him, too, if he brushed against you while he was invisible. Or gave you a nip. Just because he's invisible doesn't mean he isn't *solid*. I mean he couldn't walk through a wall or anything. He can still be shut in. Otherwise how would I get him to stay in the box when I was giving him the visibility charge?"

McGurk nodded, nodded, nodded. The way his eyes were gleaming told me two things. Not only was he completely convinced. His mind was racing ahead with other plans for the machine.

"Uh—it's *safe*, is it?" he asked.

"Well, sure," said Brains, looking troubled again. "Apart from—well . . . . There *is* just one snag, of course."

"Oh?"

"Nothing *very* serious." Brains patted the lid of the box. "You see, most people, when they think of invisibility rays, they expect to use tremendous voltages, right?"

"Right!" said Willie. "Like in the movies. Big flashes and crackling and—and—yeah! You're right, Brains."

"I used to think so myself," said Brains. "But this accident has told me different. Just a few simple flashlight batteries. That's all you need. So long as the rest of the circuit is correct."

He lifted the lid and gave us another glimpse of the colored wires and things.

"And I'm beginning to think we need even fewer batteries," he went on. "Since the snag cropped up."

"What snag exactly?" asked Wanda.

"Well, this is where it *does* get like the Invisible Man movies," said Brains. "You see, even after I bring Dennis back to full visibility, he has spells of invisibility again. *Without* the machine. Like just now, when he got into your basement."

"Oh, you poor, poor thing!" cried Wanda, clutching the dog to her chest again.

"Also he gets patchy spells," said Brains, still frowning. "Sometimes just his head disappears. Sometimes only his tail and back legs are left visible. Sometimes only the head. But don't worry," he added quickly, when it looked as if Wanda would make the dog invisible all by herself, by lovingly crushing him into a fine powder. "I think I have the answer."

"Ah!" cried McGurk.

During all this talk about the snag, McGurk had started to look doubtful, and worried, and even a bit scared. Now his whole face brightened again.

"Hey, look, Brains—how long will it take to put it right?"

Brains shrugged.

"Oh, not long. Maybe today. Certainly by tomorrow."

"Great!" said McGurk. "Just great! And then it'll be perfectly safe, right?"

"Sure," said Brains.

"And—and maybe it wouldn't take you long then to make a bigger model?"

"Well, no. I guess not."

"I mean like big enough for making a *kid* invisible. Huh? Like—*like an Invisible Investigator Machine?*"

We stared at him. We might have expected

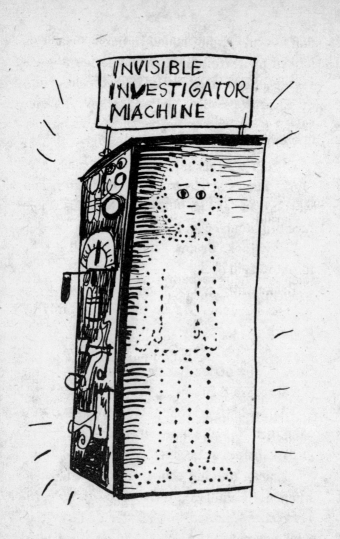

that idea to come leaping out of his head.
Even so, it still took us by surprise.

Brains was the first to recover.

Smiling sadly, he shook his head.

"Sorry, McGurk," he said. "I'd have to be
in charge of the machine at all times."

"But you *would,* man! Sure you would!
You'd be a member of the Organization. Joey,
type Gerald an I.D. card right away."

Gerald!

McGurk wasn't taking any chances with
nicknames. Now that he wanted the young
scientist's help so badly, he didn't even dare
risk calling him Brains!

But—Gerald or Brains—the kid was still
shaking his head.

"Forget it," he said. "I can understand the
way you feel, McGurk. But you don't really
want *me* in your Organization. You've told
me that a million times. You just want the
machine . . . don't you?"

We all dropped our eyes. Even McGurk
had started to blush a little. And he's no liar,
when really challenged.

"Well—I guess—in a way—maybe—" He
took a deep breath.

"But all that was *before,* Br-er—Gerald. Now, after this, I can really see how good you are. Just the sort of guy we need."

Brains smiled so sweetly I almost started thinking of him as Gerald myself. But he was still shaking his head.

"Thanks, McGurk," he said. "But no thanks. . . . And now I must get to work on the circuit. Come, Dennis."

Then he picked up the box and left us staring after him for the second time that day.

7

Lost—One Invisible Dog

We spent the next half-hour back in the basement, trying to figure out how to make Brains change his mind.

"We could threaten to tell Miss Bellingham," McGurk said, after a while. "She loves that dog and she'd go out of her mind if she heard he'd been experimenting with Dennis."

Willie looked hopeful; but Wanda would have no part of it.

"That's blackmail, McGurk! That's a crime in itself. Fine thing—a detective organization falling back on crime to get its own way!"

I agreed. Even Willie was nodding and frowning now. And McGurk sighed and muttered something about its being only an *idea*.

"I mean *someone's* got to think up ideas or we'll never get anywhere," he said, glaring around at us. "So let's hear some of yours."

Wanda said:

"Well, the way I see it is that Brains has a right to feel that way. He's been treated badly. Especially by *you*, McGurk."

"So?"

"So I think you should apologize. Properly. Handsomely. And in writing."

"What?"

McGurk looked as if he were going to come out of his rocking chair like a pilot out of an ejector seat. Fly right out of it, straight for Wanda's throat.

"Hold it!" I said. "You're right, McGurk." I turned to Wanda. "I mean, don't you see that that in itself was the most handsome apology McGurk could possibly make? By offering to let Brains *join?*"

"So all right then," said Wanda. "So what idea do *you* have?"

I sat back. I gave it my best shot.

"I think we could simply say we'll tell *everyone* about his secret. If he won't share it with us, as a member of the Organization."

"That isn't far from blackmail, either," said Wanda.

"I meant without mentioning Dennis, so he wouldn't get into trouble with his aunt. He still wouldn't like it. Not until he's perfected the machine, anyway. But it wouldn't be *nasty* like blackmail. . . . No?"

McGurk was shaking his head now.

"No, Joey. You see, if the news did get around, the Government would soon pick it up. They'd step in and take over his invention. Think of the use *they* could make of it."

"Well it *is* our Government," I said. "Maybe they've a right to know."

"Sure," said McGurk. "But not before *we've* had a chance to use it. I mean—gosh!" His eyes went glassy and dreamy. "I want to volunteer to be the first human to try it. It would make me like the first man to walk on the moon."

"Yes," said Wanda. "But they brought *him* back, don't forget."

That took a bit of the glow out of Mc-Gurk's cheeks.

"Anyway," he said, "Joey's idea isn't any good either. Any more?"

Willie sniffed. He did this the way some people clear their throats before they have an important suggestion to make.

"Yes, Willie?"

"Well—I was just thinking. I mean—well —couldn't we *pay* him to join?"

This time everyone jeered at the idea.

"What *with?*"

"Peanuts?"

"Leftover cookies from the picnic?"

Willie hung his head.

"It was only a thought," he said.

It was Brains himself who came up with the solution. Or, rather, he came *down* with it, right to the door of the basement.

"Hey, guys!" he said, huffing and puffing,

with his glasses askew and his cheeks all red. "I need help! Quick!"

"What is it?" said McGurk. He'd started to frown. I think he was all set to tell Brains to get lost. But he must have sensed an opportunity here. "Tell us about it, Gerald."

"It—it's Dennis," said Brains, holding onto the door. He's gone. You've got to help me find him."

"Well . . ." said McGurk, looking doubtful. "I'm not sure—"

"For Pete's sake," said Brains, "you're detectives, aren't you? Don't you read your own dumb notices?"

He thumped the one on the door.

It said:

HEADQUARTERS
KEEP OUT

THE McGURK
ORGANIZATION
****
PRIVATE INVESTIGATIONS
MYSTERIES SOLVED
PERSONS PROTECTED
MISSING PERSONS FOUND

We'd added that last line after solving the mystery of the Nervous Newsboy. Brains gave it an extra thump.

"What's wrong?" he snarled. "Dennis doesn't rate as a person? That it?"

"No, of course not!" said Wanda, beginning to glare at McGurk herself.

"That isn't the problem," said McGurk. "Sure we'd be glad to look for him, Brains. But he can't be classed as missing. Not in *this* short time."

"Not if he was a normal dog, you dumdum!" Brains raged. "But he'd just turned *invisible* again when he took off. I mean this is a missing *invisible* person!"

We all stared. Sure enough, this made it a whole new ball game. McGurk was already on his feet.

"I see what you mean, Brains," he said.

"He could get run over by a car?" cried Wanda. "Being invisible and all. I mean how can a driver know to avoid a dog when he can't even *see* it?"

"Right, right!" said McGurk. He patted Brains's shoulder. "Just leave it to us. . . .

There's just one thing, though. The question of a fee."

"Anything!" cried Brains. "I'll give you anything I have."

"Your membership, Gerald? You'll join the Organization?"

"You've got it!" said Brains, starting to drag McGurk out through the door. "Only *hurry!* Please! Before it's too late."

8 The Search

The scene out in the streets during the next hour was the strangest that had ever taken place in our neighborhood.

I mean, picture it yourself.

Leading the search was this little shrimp of a kid with great round glasses and a worried look, his face getting redder all the time. Stooping and cupping his hands to his ears and closing his eyes. Searching with his eyes *shut!* And every so often yelling:

"Over here! I heard his tag jingle!"

Or:

"I just felt him! He brushed my leg! He's moving your way!"

And all the time calling, calling, calling.

"Dennis! . . . Here, Dennis! . . . Good boy! . . . Doughnuts, boy!"

We let Brains do the leading like this, because Dennis would know his voice best, and therefore be more likely to respond to it than to any of ours.

Next, add to the scene four other searchers, all silent, all busy in their own ways.

One of them—the tall thin one with the long nose—was staggering around, almost on his hands and knees, sniffing like some kind of dog himself.

Another—the one with red hair and freckles and green eyes—had had the bright idea of using a very visible dog. This was Sammy, the Henshaws' beagle, always ready for a game. As soon as Sammy had spotted the strange goings-on he'd come scampering up, yelping with glee. I was all prepared to shoo him off, but McGurk said no.

"Leave him be. If *he* gets wind of an invisible dog, he'll be sure to give a sign."

Well, Sammy was giving signs, all right.

He was giving nothing else *but* signs.

He leaped in the air. He darted from one

person to another. He barked. He rolled on his back. He snatched a handkerchief out of Willie's hand. (It was there because Willie has to keep his nose clear all the time he's on a delicate sniffing mission.) In other words, Sammy simply behaved like Sammy.

"Even so," McGurk muttered at one point, "you never know. I'm sticking with him."

As for the other two members of the Organization, Wanda and I were acting even crazier. Wanda's main concern was for Dennis's safety. The thing about cars and drivers had really gotten to her. So every time a car came into a section of a street near where Brains had last heard a jingle or felt a furry body brush his leg, Wanda would step out and flag the driver down.

"Please," she would say, "please go very slow just here. We've lost—a pet."

She knew better than to say the pet was an invisible dog, in case they thought she was kidding and drove right on. But none of them suspected that. They must have thought it was some tiny creature like a gerbil or a brown mouse or a miniature turtle or something.

Anyway, they were all very kind and patient and willing to crawl along behind us while Wanda and I covered every inch of the way, bending and sweeping our arms near the surface of the road, like we were doing the breaststroke.

There was even one guy—the driver of a home heating-oil tanker truck—who backed away altogether, saying he'd make his delivery later, when he hoped we'd have found our pet.

"I had a snake myself once," he explained, chewing on his unlit cigar. "Name of Sylvester. And when he got outa the yard and was run over by a truck I cried for a week."

Not everybody was as kind and polite as the drivers, however. Other kids especially. *They* thought it was one big laugh. Burt Rafferty and his buddies soon came to jeer at us.

"Now I know you really *are* nuts, Mc-Gurk!"

"Lookit! Joey Rockaway and Wanda Grieg having a swimming race on dry land!"

"Hey! Get Willie Sandowsky! He thinks he's a Labrador!"

Sandra Ennis laughed herself sick—too

hysterical even to make any cracks of her own.

And it wasn't just old enemies who gathered around to laugh, either. Kids we thought of as friends—even some of those we'd helped in the past—all had stupid grins on their faces and kept tapping their foreheads. I mean, who could blame them? We couldn't explain. If we'd said we were trying to catch an invisible dog, they'd only have laughed and jeered louder than ever.

"Just ignore them," McGurk kept muttering, whenever he and Sammy came dashing into earshot. "They'll laugh on the other side of their faces when they know the real truth."

Then Mrs. McGurk came and put an end to it all.

We'd just worked our way back around to the street in front of McGurk's house, when his mother came out with the message. Not for him. For Brains. Being used to McGurk's stunts, she paid no attention to our strange behavior and got right to the point.

"Oh, Gerald," she said, "your aunt's just called from New York."

"Oh yes, Mrs. McGurk?" he said, blinking up from his inspection of a bush at the side of the driveway. "There's nothing wrong, I hope?"

Mrs. McGurk smiled and shook her head.

"No. She was just a bit worried when she called her own number a few minutes ago and you weren't there to answer it. I told her you were playing with Jack and his friends."

"Oh. Good. Thanks."

Brains looked polite enough, but you could tell he was burning to get on with the search.

"She also wanted to make sure that Dennis—"

Mrs. McGurk stopped and looked around.

"Where is he, by the way? I thought I heard you calling his name."

"Uh—no—he's O.K. He's in the house," said Brains, blushing a little—as well he might!

"Yes. Well. Your aunt asked me to make sure that Dennis had been fed this morning. You *did* feed him?"

"Oh—Yes. Sure."

"I thought so. I told her you were a very reliable boy. Not like some I can mention.

. . . She also wanted to know if you found the salad she'd left in the refrigerator for your lunch."

"Yes, yes—thanks."

Brains was looking hunted.

McGurk, who'd been looking hurt at his mother's crack about reliability, now seemed positively angry.

"That's all right then," said Mrs. McGurk, completely ignoring all these signs of uneasiness. "Mind you don't get into any mischief."

Then she went back into the house.

"Right!" said Brains, after releasing a big long sigh. "So now let's get on with the search. I think I heard him across the street just then."

We all turned, ready to go. All except McGurk.

"Wait!" he said to us three members of the Organization. There was a peculiar gleam in his eyes. He managed to switch it off and smile as he turned to Brains. "Gerald," he said, "why don't you go ahead on your own for a while? Get some of these rubberneckers to help you."

Brains frowned.

"Well—sure. But why? Where are you go-ing? I thought you wanted to help."

"Oh, but we do, we do!" said McGurk, still with the rather tight smile on his face. "It's just that I think we've been going about it the wrong way. This search needs careful planning. Systematic. Scientific. *You* know. That's the way the McGurk Organization usually gets results. So I'm taking my staff back to HQ, where we can work out a proper ground plan, with maps and all. We'll see you later."

"But—"

"Later, Gerald. It's the best way." When McGurk turned to us, the hard green gleam was back. "Come on, men. Right now."

As we followed him into the basement, I said:

"But what's the idea, McGurk? We'll just be wasting our time."

"Yes," said Wanda, "with Dennis in ter-rible danger with every minute that goes by."

McGurk wouldn't speak until he'd closed the door behind us. Firmly. Then he said, in a low grim voice:

"Wasting time, huh? And what do you

think we've been doing all afternoon?" No
smile now. He loked mad. Absolutely furious.
"That—that owl-faced *creep*—he—he's been
fooling us all along!"

"Eh?"

"How?"

"What makes you think *that* all of a sudden?"

He growled.

"What made me *realize* it—*know* it—all of a sudden was my mother's message. I mean, figure it out yourselves. If his aunt wanted to know if he'd fed Dennis this morning, she must have been out all day. Right?"

We frowned, but nodded.

"Right . . . sure . . . so?"

"So remember the first time—lunchtime—after we'd chased the doughnut and he left us with the box?"

"He—gosh!"

Suddenly I'd remembered.

McGurk nodded.

"Yeah—*gosh!* He said he'd thought he'd heard his aunt call him in—up in the house. So that means he *deliberately* left us to examine that box. It was all *planned*."

"Yes," I said, thoughtfully. "But—I mean, all right. So there's a trick in this somehow. But *how?* I mean how the heck did he make it look like the dog was invisible?"

"And *sound* like it was invisible?" said Wanda.

"And *smell* like it was invisible?" said Willie, picking the bone out of the CLUES box.

McGurk thumped the table, making the file of MYSTERIES SOLVED jump to life.

"That," said McGurk, "is what we've really come back here to investigate. As of right now we're gonna look into this case like detectives instead of dummies!"

Then he gave the table another bash and made the records of our past successes shiver with indignation and rustle and whisper.

"Hear, hear!" they seemed to be saying.

The Heap of Grass

I mentioned earlier about two kinds of brains: brains good at science and math, like Gerald Bellingham's; and brains good at English and general intelligence, like mine.

Well, there are other kinds. There're the kind of brains that are good at spotting little things, especially little things that don't seem quite right. Then there're the kind of brains that will go on puzzling over these little things until they do make sense. And there're also the kind of brains that get brilliant hunches and ideas out of nowhere. Put these last three types together and what have we got?

A born detective's brains, that's what.

Like Jack P. McGurk's.

When he suddenly said we'd better start thinking like detectives instead of dummies, we listened, we became alert.

Wanda picked up the rubber bone.

"Well, this should be easy enough to plant in the furnace room, I suppose. Even through the narrow windows. He'd simply toss it in, while we were busy in here."

"Or before that," I said. "While we were out at the picnic." Then I frowned. "But that doesn't explain the jingling."

Willie sniffed.

"The smell—O.K. That was on the bone. But it doesn't explain the growling. The growling *and* the jingling. You know. When he was picking up the—uh—invisible dog. Over at the door there."

McGurk was nodding at all this.

"Don't worry, men," he said. "We'll get to that later. I have a few ideas about those points. But let's start at the beginning. The doughnut. Any ideas about *that?*"

We looked at one another, frowning and shrugging.

"Come on!" said McGurk, slapping the table. "Think! How could he get the doughnut to roll off the table and away over the grass into his aunt's yard?"

There was another pause. We were thinking, all right.

I was first to take a shot.
"I guess he could have *harpooned* it somehow. Like fired a dart at it. A dart with some strong thread attached, like a fishing line."

McGurk nodded—but doubtfully.

"He'd have to be a terrific shot, Joey. And anyway, one of us would have been sure to see the dart hit the plate of doughnuts. I mean, right under our noses!"

Suddenly Wanda had *her* idea.

"Hey! Fishing line! Yes! Maybe Joey's closer than we think. Only instead of firing it from a gun, all Brains did was get up into the tree and *fish* for the doughnut. Just come here a minute."

She had gone to the door and opened it and now she was halfway up the steps and pointing to the end of the yard.

"See that? There's a branch that runs right over where we had the table and on over to the bushes, right to Miss Bellingham's yard."

McGurk was shaking his head.

"Good try, Wanda. But Brains would have to be a better climber than *you,* even. And to dangle a fishing line over the table, while we were all sitting around it, without us *seeing* it? And then to move quietly along the branch, without disturbing the leaves, trailing the doughnut along under him? No way!"

There was another pause as we stared at the tree, and the limb, and the bushes, and the space where the table had been, and the two benches that were still there.

"But you're right about one thing, Officer Grieg," McGurk murmured. "We *should* study the scene carefully. Only forget about the tree, huh? Let's just go over what we actually *did* see. Come on. . . ."

Then he had us sit on the benches in the same places: himself and Willie on one side, facing Wanda and me on the other. And since this turned out to be so important, I've made this plan of it for our files:

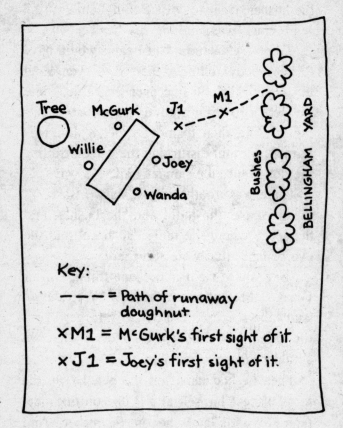

Tree

McGurk

J1
×

M1
×

YARD

Willie

Joey

Wanda

Bushes

BELLINGHAM

Key:

— — — = Path of runaway
          doughnut.

×M1 = McGurk's first sight of it.

×J1 = Joey's first sight of it.

"Now," said McGurk. "Who saw the doughnut first?"

"You were the first to shout, McGurk," Wanda said.

"Right," said McGurk. He got up and walked halfway to the bushes. Then he kicked the grass with his heel. "Just about here. Maybe a bit farther on."

I cleared my throat.

"I—uh—saw it before that," I confessed. "Out of the corner of my eye. I didn't say anything because I thought it was a trick of the light at first." I got up. "And that was nearer the table," I said. "Just about here."

McGurk came over. He was staring hard at the ground near my feet. Then he suddenly stiffened—and pounced.

"Bingo!" he cried, straightening up with a handful of loose grass clippings, from a small heap there.

"What is it?"

"What's it look like? Loose grass, you dummies!" The look of joy left McGurk's face and a most sinister sly and leering expression replaced it. He was really getting going now! "But—" he went on, casting a

91

gloating glance over to the bushes—"our mower doesn't leave any loose grass. Our mower has a sack on it, and it all goes in there. Besides—" he took a closer look at the clippings—"this looks green—freshly cut, and we haven't cut ours in a week. So what's it doing here? I'll tell you. Brains *put* it here. Earlier. *Before* the picnic."

We stared at the small pile of cut grass among the McGurk's rougher grass. Now that our attention had been drawn to it, we could see McGurk was right. Otherwise—well—it was no wonder none of us had noticed it before, including McGurk. It was the perfect camouflage for a concealed doughnut.

"But—so what?" mumbled Willie.

"I know!" I said. "It was to hide the doughnut in, right, McGurk?"

"Right. One of his aunt's doughnuts, probably. Probably long before we'd even set the table. A doughnut already tied to a long length of thread. Fine nylon thread. Which was green, I bet."

I frowned. I'd just thought of something.

"How would he know to use a doughnut, though? I mean, how would he know we'd be having them at the picnic?"

"That's easy!" Wanda said. "He probably heard *you*, McGurk, bragging about our plans for the picnic. You've been doing it for days." She turned to me. "Sure, Brains would know we'd be having doughnuts. I bet he knew the whole menu. So he'd have all the time in the world to get *that* particular doughnut ready."

"I still don't see—" Willie began.

"No," said McGurk. *"None* of us saw. Until Brains started to pull on it, and draw it out of this covering of grass. *Then* we saw it. *Then* we couldn't believe our eyes. *Then* we were all softened up, ready and ripe to believe in an invisible dog."

We were nodding. Even Willie. It was beginning to make sense. But there were still some pretty tough problems.

"What about the jingling, though?" I said. "Do you figure—?"

"Same principle," said McGurk. "Nylon thread again. Let's take a look at *that* scene."

He led the way back into the basement and through to the furnace room.

"All he had to do," said McGurk, "was dangle some dog tags through the window and shake them."

But this time Wanda objected.

"Not so fast, McGurk. I mean we'd have seen them. Like we saw the doughnut. As he pulled them back up. Especially the second time, when we all turned so quickly from the bone as soon as we heard the jingling."

"No! Hey! Uh—*no!*" Willie was way in front for once. "Not if he just let them lie on the floor. We wouldn't see them then. All this junk."

"Good thinking, Willie!" McGurk looked pleased. "Let's take a look now—and I bet you we'll find those metal tags lying here."

But no. He was wrong that time. There were no dog tags or pieces of chain or anything like that. Only the same old litter: scraps of paper, a few playing cards, a few thousand dollars in Monopoly money, the scattered nails—

"The nails! Of *course!*"

Even as I'd been dismissing them, McGurk had pounced, and was crouching down.

"Come on, men! Pick 'em up! Let's see if any—"

"*Hey!*"

That was Wanda.

She'd picked up one of the nails and a whole little bunch of five or six came with it. They were strung close together with a fine gray thread we hadn't noticed, and there was a long trail of it after that—long enough to dangle the bunch from the window and close to the floor.

"Listen!" said Wanda, giving them a shake.

It was the same jingle, all right.

McGurk seemed to purr. His eyes glowed and his grin broadened.

"Oh, boy!" he said. "That Brains! I've got to hand it to him! He's really something else!"

I brought him back to reality.

"Yes," I said. "Sure. But the dog noises, McGurk. Aren't you forgetting *them?* The growling *as well as* the jingling? When he pretended to pick Dennis up?"

McGurk frowned.

"Yes. Well. There *is* a slight problem there. I think I know how he did it, but—"

"A ventriloquist trick, McGurk?" said Wanda. "Brains is a ventriloquist?" She sighed. "I thought of that, too. But he'd have to be really first-rate. I mean I was watching his face. He was talking to the—uh—invisible dog all the time the jingling and growling was going on. I mean think about it. What ventriloquist can speak with three voices at the same time?"

McGurk was shaking his head slowly.

"No, no, Wanda. Ventriloquist nothing! You're forgetting the kind of guy our suspect is. He's a scientist. He knows how to handle all kinds of electronic gadgets. My guess is that he was using a tape recorder. He recorded the noises earlier and switched them on when he was pretending to grab the dog. Only . . . ." His face clouded. "Where would he hide it? A thing like that would make too big a bulge if he'd stuffed it under his shirt. And it would be too big to slip into any of his pockets."

"Oh no it wouldn't!"

Willie was smiling, looking more confident then I'd ever seen him before.

McGurk was startled.

"Eh? How do *you* know?"

"Because my dad has one he slips into *his* pocket easy enough. It's only as big as a small electric shaver, and it runs on batteries."

"A *tape recorder?*"

"Yeah. Well. Same kind of thing. He calls it an electronic notepad. They use them in some offices all the time."

"He's right," I said. "Like a scratch pad, only you speak into it instead of write on it. Then you play it back when you want to refer to your notes. I'm hoping to get one myself next Christmas."

McGurk clapped his hands together. He was all smiles again.

"Well that's *it* then! The guy had it all planned down to the last detail. And when it was backed up by that phony machine, with all that fancy wiring, it's no wonder he had us believing it."

Wanda didn't look quite so triumphant.

"Yes, but what *about* that box? I mean we saw it empty. Then he presses the switches and things and lifts the lid—and there's Dennis inside!"

McGurk grinned.

"The switches and things you can forget. They were all a blind. The big lever, maybe not."

"How do you mean?"

"Because he'd have to have something to operate the false bottom. To close it down to hide the dog, to lift it up to show the dog. It's just a routine magician's thing. Brains could fix up something like that in his sleep. And Dennis—well, I told you right at the start how well trained *he* is."

"Well, I'll be darned!" I murmured, seeing it all fit into place. "I could kick myself."

"Me, too!"

"And me!"

"Don't feel so bad about it, men. Remember it had even *me* fooled. If we hadn't been dazzled by all those wires and batteries and labels and switches, we'd probably have thought of it right away. Anyway, let's see if the box is lying around anywhere in Miss Bellingham's yard now. I'd like to check on it. Just to wrap up the case nice and tidy."

10

"Here's our big chance!"

Stealthily, we made our way to the bushes. Stealthily, because we'd heard voices. And no—the "Invisibility Machine" wasn't there, over in Miss Bellingham's yard. But Brains and Dennis were, and so was Miss Bellingham.

Miss Bellingham isn't a bit like her nephew.

She is a big woman—not fat, but very tall and bulky. According to McGurk, she is so *un*scientific-minded that she sometimes has trouble operating a can opener. The only thing she shares with Brains is her weak eyesight. She wears large thick glasses, too, only on her they look small.

She has a strong voice, though. It was booming out now, as she bent over the boy and the dog.

"And have you both been good while I was away?"

"Yurrip!" said Dennis.

"Oh yes, Aunt Christine!" said Brains.

"Huh!" grunted McGurk.

"But you weren't in when I called, were you?" Miss Bellingham boomed, a bit accusingly.

"No, but we were only out in the yard here, Aunt Christine. I was fixing this new tether for Dennis, you see."

"A tether?"

We all peered closer through the leaves. We were as curious as Miss Bellingham sounded. I mean *we* knew what he'd been doing. We were just curious to see how smart he could be with his excuses.

"Yes," he was explaining, running a hand along a length of clothes cord. He'd fixed one end to the wall of the house, about two feet from the ground, and the other to a stump at the end of the yard, same height. "A tether."

He took Dennis to the stump. There was a leash fixed to the little dog's collar now. Then, as his aunt watched, blinking in a puzzled kind of way, Brains unhooked the cord from the stump. slipped it through the loop at the end of Dennis's leash, then hooked the cord onto the stump again.

"There!" he said. "Off you go, boy!"

Dennis hesitated a few seconds.

"Go on! Go! commanded Brains.

Then off Dennis trotted up the yard—free to move where he wanted in either direction up or down, but only as far as the leash would let him from side to side.

"How clever!" boomed Miss Bellingham. "He's a good dog and he'd never stray from the yard normally. But now I can leave him

when I'm away for the day and be absolutely sure he's all right. A brilliant idea, Gerald!"

"Big deal!" muttered Wanda. "They taught us that in Care of Pets at the Brownies."

But Miss Bellingham had obviously never been a Brownie.

"Brilliant!" she boomed again.

Even Brains didn't have the gall to accept all that praise.

"Well, it's an old idea really, Aunt. Not one of my originals. But Dennis loves it."

"He certainly does! You clever boy! You deserve what I brought back for you from the city after all. Come along. I can't wait to show it to you now."

Brains looked as if he couldn't wait either, as he went hurrying after his long-striding aunt. She was known to be a big spender as far as gifts for her only nephew were concerned.

Dennis was left wandering happily up and down the yard, tethered to the cord, sniffing and jingling.

"I hope whatever it is she brought him was broken on the way back," said Willie, shocked by Brains's coolness after all he'd put us through.

"Yes," said Wanda. "He deserves—"

But McGurk cut her short. *He* wasn't frowning sullenly. His eyes had their brightest gleam yet.

"Right, men!" he said. "Here's our big chance!"

"What for?"

"To pay back old Brains, that's what for. With interest!"

11 The Return of the Invisible Dog

It didn't take long.

Dennis was used to us by now. He made no fuss when McGurk snuck into the yard, un-hitched the end of the cord from the stump, and slipped the loop of the leash free. In fact the little dog just wagged his stumpy tail, and he went on wagging it and licking Wanda's face as she carried him back to our HQ.

"Now we just wait!" murmured McGurk, listening at the slightly open door.

That didn't take long either.

About five minutes, I made it.

Then:

"Dennis! Dennis! Here, boy! Dennis!"

In a strange croaky whisper.

"He won't want his aunt to know her pet has gotten free from his stupid tether," said McGurk. "But he's getting desperate. Just listen."

"Dennis! Hey—doughnuts, boy! Juicy marrow bones Dennis, boy—*please!*"

We followed McGurk out into the yard then. I closed the door behind us carefully.

"Hey! You guys seen anything of Dennis?" croaked Brains.

He was on the McGurk side of the bushes, looking around, bewildered.

"How *can* we see anything of Dennis?" said McGurk. "When he's invisible?"

"And lost somewhere out in the streets," said Wanda.

Brains's face went through five or six different expressions inside two seconds. Then he swallowed and said:

"He—he came back. I was meaning to tell you. He's visible again. But he's also gone off again! Oh, gosh—and my aunt's back and—"

"We know he's gone off again," said McGurk, grimly.

"Eh? I thought you just said you hadn't seen him."

"We haven't. All we saw was *this!*"

Still with the grim look, McGurk brought out Dennis's leash and collar from behind his back.

Brains goggled.

"We saw them streaking across our lawn," said McGurk. "Just the leash at first, like a snake. We guessed there was Dennis at the

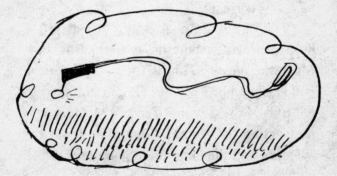

end of it and he'd gone invisible again. So I grabbed at the leash and tugged and—well—he must have slipped his collar as well. Because suddenly *it* appeared too, from under the invisible hair."

Brains was still staring. But now a strange wobbly grin began to creep across his face.

"Ah, come on, McGurk! That invisible stuff—that was just a trick!"

McGurk acted shocked. Correction. Being McGurk, he overacted shocked. He gasped. He staggered back. He gaped. I thought he was going to blow it.

"A *what?* You mean the Invisibility Machine was just a—a—"

Brains was too worried to judge McGurk's behavior correctly.

"Yes!" he said impatiently. "It was just a box with a false bottom. A trick. But, hey, McGurk, *please!* This is for real. Where've you stashed him? My aunt'll go mad if—"

"But—*false bottom? Trick?*" McGurk was now acting bewildered. "But what about the switches and the lamp and the batteries?"

"That was just to make it look good. To

distract your attention. Hey, now, come on! Cut it out and—"

"But no. Seriously. Hold it, Brains." McGurk was now acting astonished. "We didn't know that. We still thought—gosh!" He turned to me. "Joey, could it be another of those accidental discoveries in science? Like you were telling us about. Could Brains have *stumbled* onto this invisibility thing?"

"Like the discovery of penicillin?" I said. "And inoculation? And the law of gravity? And—"

"And gunpowder?" said Willie.

Brains knew enough about these things to be pulled up by our words. He probably knew more about them—and many other accidental science discoveries—than we did. His face had grown very pale.

"Oh, *no!*" he groaned. "Oh, my *gosh!*" He stared at us. "You mean you really did see just the leash and collar running around, and —oh, *no!*"

Then we couldn't help it. The look on his face was so pathetic. We just broke up laughing.

Then we led him into the basement and

showed him Dennis playing happily with his rubber bone, and then Brains laughed too—laughed and laughed until huge magnified tears began to roll from behind those powerful glasses.

12 The Fifth Member

And that's how the McGurk Organization got its fifth member.

After we'd finished laughing, and Dennis had had his collar put back, and we'd told Brains just how we'd figured it all out at last, McGurk said:

114

"Brains, the offer still stands. If you want to join the Organization."

Brains was just wiping the last of the tears from his face. His smile faded.

"Huh? But—but all you wanted me for was my Invisibility Machine."

"Then," said McGurk. "Yes. But any guy who can work out a stunt like that, *and pull it off*—well, he's worth a place in our Organization any time. For his own sake. Right, men?"

"Right!"

"No question!"

"You bet!"

Brains blinked at us. For a second or two, I thought the tears were going to spurt out again. Then he grinned.

"Well," he said, "I guess any Organization that can figure all that out and then give the joker the scare of his life with his own joke— I guess that organization is *worth* joining."

"Great!" said McGurk. "Joey, just type out—"

But Brains hadn't finished.

"And you know, McGurk—fellow officers —I really can be a big help with science problems. I mean I may not be too good at shadowing or searching for clues or arresting suspects—but, well, I can make you some devices to help *you* do the shadowing. Like periscopes, for instance. And rearview sunglasses. And I can dig out a whole lot of hidden information from the clues you find. With my microscope and my chemistry sets. And—and when you catch a suspect I can fix two kinds of lie detectors. One that bleeps or one that flickers. And then there are chemicals for four different kinds of invisible ink. And another chemical that's invisible at first but then stains the fingers of anyone touching—"

"Fine! Fine!" McGurk was almost drooling at these mentions of scientific aids. He couldn't wait to get Brains signed up now, before he changed his mind. "So you're in charge of the McGurk Organization's new crime lab. Joey, see that this information is typed on Gerald's I.D. card. And don't forget to leave a space for his signature."

"There's just one thing," murmured Brains wistfully, as I reached for my typewriter.

He suddenly looked much more like a kid than a scientist now. A little shrimp of a nine-year-old, going on ten.

"What's that?" asked McGurk anxiously, no doubt wondering if the deal was going to fall through.

"I've joined just too late for the McGurk Organization's Annual Picnic."

McGurk's face cleared.

"No problem, Officer Bellingham. We'll have another one tomorrow."

Brains the Kid looked delighted for a second. Then Brains the Scientist frowned.

"But an *annual* picnic means—"

"You're as bad as Joey," sighed McGurk. "Listen. All of you. Today's McGurk Organization Annual Picnic was for the four members belonging to it at that time. Right?"

"Well—uh—right."

"Sure—I guess."

"Right!" said McGurk, surging on. "So tomorrow we're going to have the McGurk Organization Annual Picnic for the *five* members belonging to it *now*. Anything wrong with that?"

There wasn't.

Not a single thing.

As I said before: Jack P. McGurk has a special kind of brain all his own.

ABOUT THE AUTHOR
AND ILLUSTRATOR

E. W. HILDICK has written over forty children's books. Archway Paperback editions include *A Cat Called Amnesia*, *The Top-Flight, Fully-Automated Junior High School Girl Detective*, and the *McGurk Mystery* series, which now has seven titles: *Deadline for McGurk*, *The Case of the Condemned Cat*, *The Case of the Nervous Newsboy*, *The Great Rabbit Rip-off*, *The Case of the Invisible Dog*, *The Case of the Secret Scribbler*, and *The Case of the Phantom Frog*. Mr. Hildick's books have been published in over a dozen countries. A British subject, he and his wife divide their time between homes in England and the United States.

LISL WEIL, who has been writing and illustrating for many years, has over eighty children's books to her credit. Each year Ms. Weil performs at Young People's Concerts with major symphony orchestras, illustrating a story in the rhythm of the music. She lives in New York City.